A SOLAR FLARE

A SOLAR FLARE

CANDACE R. NUNAG

TUSCALOOSA

Copyright © 2025 by Candace R. Nunag
The University of Alabama Press
Tuscaloosa, Alabama 35487-0380
All rights reserved
FC2 is an imprint of the University of Alabama Press

Inquiries about reproducing material from this work should be addressed to the University of Alabama Press

Book Design: Publications Unit, Department of English, Illinois State University; Director: Steve Halle, Production Assistant: Jalissa Jones
Cover design: Matthew Revert
Typeface: Hypatia Sans Pro

Lyrics from "Away from the Roll of the Sea"—words and music by Allister MacGillivray, Cabot Trail Music (SOCAN)—are used by permission.

Library of Congress Cataloging-in-Publication Data is available from the Library of Congress.
ISBN: 978-1-57366-210-9
E-ISBN: 978-1-57366-913-9

For Steven

This is a history of telegraphy. This is a history of suicidality. This is a history of a cathedral. This is a history of women's handbags. This is a history of being dragged out, kicking and screaming. This is a history of the boogeyman. This is a history of Wellbutrin. This is a history of the Cold War. This is a history of information technology. This is a history of biracial subjectivity. This is a history of microgravity. This is a history of the digital texture of connection.

—

To be sung out loud:
Small craft in a harbor, that's still and serene
Give no indication what their ways have been
They rock at their moorings all nestled in dreams
Away from the roll of the sea

I have dreams where I wake up and don't use my smartphone. And it's not that I just don't use it, it's that the phone isn't there at all—as though it has gone away because I have surpassed the need for it.

I cried once, thinking about how I will probably wake up every day of my life and feel the need to check my email—thinking that I'll probably die with a phone on my nightstand.

But I only cried just that one time.

Google makes money by observing our observing. Each of our searches and clicks are aggregated, recorded, and then sold to advertisers. The advertisers use the information to deploy highly specific marketing to our browsers and email inboxes. Every time we google something, we are performing unpaid labor.

In the same vein, social media sites like Facebook, Instagram, and X, formerly known as Twitter, foster a digital environment for a novel, late-capitalist subject called the "prosumer." A prosumer is an individual who both consumes *and* produces content on a social media platform, thus performing unpaid labor in two ways at once.

The social media of my past lives.

I am currently in pursuit of the silhouette of an archive. I am currently making my own samsara. Just the extant tape, tacks, nails, and staples on telephone poles, lampposts, and stoplights. I am currently making my own samsara. I am currently in pursuit of the razor-thin shadow of a paper trail. I am currently making my own samsara. Just the evidence that someone, anyone, had a message worthy of at least one other person. I am currently making my own samsara. I am currently in pursuit of the footprint of our primordial desire to connect with another. I am currently making my own samsara. Just the tokens left behind before our archives stopped casting shadows.

Writing is an important gesture, because it both articulates and produces that state of mind which is called "historical consciousness." History began with the invention of writing, not for the banal reason often advanced that written texts permit us to reconstruct the past, but for the mere pertinent reason that the world is not perceived as a process, "historically," unless one signifies it by successive symbols, by writing. The difference between prehistory and history is not that we have written documents which permit us to read the second, but that during history there are literate men who experience, understand, and evaluate the world as a "becoming," while in prehistory no such existential attitude is possible. If the art of writing were to fall into oblivion, or if it were to become subservient to picture making, (as in the so-called "script-writing" in films), history in the strict sense of that term would be over.

—Vilém Flusser, 1987

When I was eighteen and my brother was nineteen, I made a Facebook account. My brother was troubled and had a difficult time graduating from high school, so he didn't go off to college the way that I did. Accordingly, he was not afforded the luxury of a Facebook account, which at the time you could only procure with a university email address. He killed himself the second day of my second semester, having never made a Facebook page.

Having lived with the Facebook account for as long as I have lived without him, I am puzzled by friends posting on the walls of the deceased on their death anniversaries, even more so on their birthdays.

Did I lose him twice? Am I still losing him right now?

The Carrington Event of 1859 refers to a solar storm and flare that fried much of the relatively new telegraph system across the globe. The surge of magnetized particles burned up all the skinny little strips of paper attached to the telegraph machines. The flare also caused aurora borealis as far south as the Tropic of Cancer.

This is the evidence of absence. This is substantial nothingness.

When he opened the door, he was greeted with an unusual smell, though this did not alarm him. The bouquet was familiar, and he would have regarded it earlier in the un-evening had he needed the kindling. Nonetheless, he knew it would be strange to return to work so soon and for unprecedented reasons, so the aroma seemed harmonious with regard to the circumstances. The curiousness of the situation was such that he remained quite aloof when, by oscillating light, he discerned the scorch marks and ash that littered the office.

Very few young boys grow up dreaming of becoming electric telegraphists. He thought now that even fewer would, since the world would soon become acutely aware of just how fragile their implements are. He felt a pang of dolefulness affixed to the sad irony of the night's toil: if the receiver would obey him, it would only serve to insult his métier. Alas, there was work to be done and transmissions to send.

It was difficult to rest with the gasping fervor on the first night, but tonight, the second night, the onlookers only looked. With the looming monotony of catch-up work, he thought it might have been nice to have some audible ardor out on the street, if only to keep him awake.

Nevertheless, he considered himself lucky: it was easier to work by the light of the auroras.

Basic qualifications for NASA astronauts

—Pass the long-duration spaceflight physical:
- 20/20 vision (can be corrected to 20/20)
- Blood pressure of 140/90
- Minimum height of 5'2", maximum 6'3"

—Successful completion of (at least) a bachelor's degree in a biological or physical science, engineering, or math

If selected, astronaut candidates train for one to two years at the Johnson Space Center in Houston, Texas. Within one month of the start of the training, astronaut candidates are required to complete a swimming test that includes the ability to tread water for ten continuous minutes, as well as swim seventy-five meters fully clothed in a flight suit and sneakers. Prior to starting the flight and extravehicular activity components of the training, astronaut candidates must also become scuba certified and complete a military water-survival protocol.

In a class discussion, one of my students reflected on the theoretical Dyson sphere, the prospect of unlimited energy for fueling digitally transcribed consciousness, and how they were unsure about whether or not they'd like to live forever—unsure if eternal digitized consciousness was a good or bad thing.

The discussion ground to a halt. I'll share the blame for this impasse: I was taken aback by the self-assuredness of the student's belief that eternal consciousness was a veritable lifestyle option out of many, laid out for one's choosing.

Once my surprise dissipated, I remembered my class roster: this student was the same age that I was when my brother died. I wondered if I would share this student's same conundrum had I not experienced existential rupture at eighteen. Would I, too, have entertained the thought of living forever had the back of my hand not grazed the specter of Death?

In the fecund silence of the lecture hall, I did the only thing a teacher could do: ask questions.

Why is it that, among some cultures and spiritualities, eternal consciousness is akin to eternal damnation? What would it mean to live forever? And is it possible that death, or endings in general, provide meaning for our lives and experiences?

The pump of a bellows—an effulgence of embers. Hands went up.

And, together, we did the only thing students can do: carry on.

Samsara is a Buddhist concept meaning the unending cycle of suffering. Suffering is caused by desire and attachments, and to live in a state of samsara is to live in constant pursuit of desires. In the Western world, the constant, if not chronic, pursuit of desire is sometimes called "the hedonic treadmill."

The United States' Declaration of Independence advocates for its citizens' samsara when it states that they are all entitled to the "pursuit of happiness."

My father's death wasn't a suicide, but it wasn't not a suicide. The polite way to put it: he died from cancer of the head and neck. The blunt way to put it: he died from two-thirds of his tongue getting cut out and the surgical-wound-turned-crater in his neck never healing. The earnest way to put it: he died by his own hand.

He killed himself drink by drink, cigarette by cigarette, over the course of eleven years, starting the day we closed his son's casket. Of course, this whole process was expedited by the summer of 2014, when his nephew and brother drank themselves to death within a few weeks of each other.

I was never under the impression that someone could be both patient and harried to make or find or meet their end. I was never under that impression until I was.

>Dad was born in 1965, and his digital footprint was less a footprint and more a stilted leap over a muddy puddle.

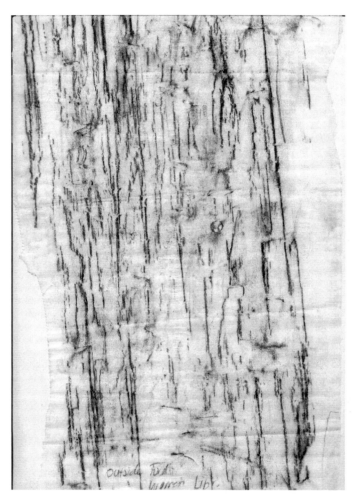

This one made my hands filthy.

The hope is that, in not too many years, human brains and computing machines will be coupled together very tightly, and that the resulting partnership will think as no human brain has ever thought and process data in a way not approached by the information-handling machines we know today.

—J. C. R. Licklider, 1960

100.01

It occurred to me in a dissociated state while operating heavy machinery that I live in a time where an email could be my swan song. Famous last words are always swimming, bathing in my poorly lit mind. I imagine a swooping, flapping, unending stream of paper, the kind with the holes on the side whose margins need be manually detached, with billions of last words. Somewhere on this feeble monumental sash, perhaps around the year 2000, the last words all start to look the same. "by EOB today." "Best, [signature with stern alphabet soup of credentialing]" "Received" "See attached."

Suicide is often talked about as though it is an unlawful offense. To "commit suicide" is to be implicitly criminal in the act of taking one's own life—the criminal act being endowing oneself with the license to kill. Perhaps the offensiveness of the transgression is exacerbated by the fact that the individual doesn't stick around long enough to carry the shame and lowly status afforded only to an executioner.

Some mental health care providers are making an effort to change how suicide is talked about in our culture. These advocates promote eschewing the phrase "committing suicide" in favor of "died by suicide."

My uncle lived three states over and I only got to see him every once in a while. One year, when my visit overlapped with his June birthday, I brought him a mint chocolate chip ice cream cake. He wore a long duster coat out to his celebratory lunch, even though it was hot and muggy, because he fancied himself a cowboy. He hugged me twice on this occasion and told me how happy he was to spend time with his niece on his birthday.

> *I am precious with this recollection of him, sheathed in late-spring humidity and his cowboy coat—especially when I try to drown out the image of the last time I saw him alive. He was in the ICU and had so many tubes and wires in and about him that he looked like what is perhaps the opposite of a cowboy: a cyborg.*

A long while after he finally expired, I was offered a scrap of wisdom:

> Fathers teach us about life, but uncles teach us how to tell stories.

In most US cities, there is a two-to-three-day delivery time for intracity but inter–zip code letters.

I saw a commercial on television with people dancing and singing in the street. They quite literally sang the praises of targeted advertising and just how good it is for sellers and buyers. I felt somehow mocked by their aplomb, then gravely concerned that their rejoicing was akin to an act of worship.

I tried to search for a YouTube video of this commercial, wherein I found only informational videos about how to instrumentalize targeted marketing.

However, in the gap dimension of this missing commercial, in its substantial nothingness, I found an idea: commercial advertisements themselves might be the most ephemeral objects on the internet.

I could hang my jacket.

For the first time in the long history of our relationship with tools and machines we have a radically different technology (the computer) based upon a radically different logic (digital) whose use and influence is so widespread and powerful that we can consider the concept that we are analogue creatures because we now have something to philosophically contrast and compare it with. In other words, before our societies became networked it made no sense to think of ourselves as analogue, because there was no ontological basis for it to be considered a problem or issue to think about in a concrete, everyday way. Now we do.

—Robert Hassan & Thomas Sutherland, 2016

Once I read the lament of a scientist who came of age in the 1970s:

He lamented his technocratic faith in progress.

He lamented that he had ever believed that science would be our species's saving grace.

He wished that he had used his energy to combat greed and capitalism.

—

To be administered in case of an emergency:
Sus/
Mari/
Osep!

I have never seen anyone die for the ontological argument.

—Albert Camus, 1942

100.02

I go out of my way to walk my letters to an actual public mailbox at whatever corner in any of the neighborhoods in which I have lived. I justify this inefficiency with my immedicable contrarianism, assuring myself that I am not a machine who should be perpetually working. But justifications are different than the truth: I drop off letters in the big blue mailboxes because in Kurt Vonnegut's memoir he describes them like frogs and says "ribbit" upon deposit of his correspondence; I gave my copy of this book to my dear cousin before he drank himself to death.

In Tibetan Buddhism, bardos are in-between spaces. The most well-known bardo is the space after death and before another life. The part of a person that makes its way through these bardos and through lifetimes is *namshe*, or a dualistic consciousness.

It is helpful to think of *namshe* less like a noun and more a like verb.

Winter sun is a bardo.

I sometimes find myself waiting for the day after his eighteenth death anniversary.

On the day that I have lived more of my life without him than with him, I might feel differently than the day before.

When photography became commercialized in the mid-nineteenth century, photographers created a cryptic slogan that perhaps represents the advent of commercialized digitization:

"Secure the shadow, while the substance yet remains."

Shadow aggregation.

100.03

Even though a therapist once told me that trauma can distort memories, I have yet to euthanize the semblance of a brother that now lives only in my mind. My recollections of him are like the bright white homes on Greek coastlines: sun-faded, desiccated but legible, and all the while there are mundane domestic happenings just past the façade. It stings my eyes to look too closely but I do it anyway, satisfying an urge I feel is id-ish but I refuse to understand. All I have left is this retinal pain and a him-shaped lacuna in my memory bank.

Karuna is a Pali word that means "the trembling or quivering of the heart in response to a being's pain."

Could there be a narcissism in grieving the death of a sibling?

Since there is no one in the world with a more similar genetic make-up, and there is no one in the world with a more similar upbringing, perhaps experiencing their death is very much like seeing one's own.

An event in a subject's life defined by its intensity, by the subject's incapacity to respond adequately to it, and by the upheaval and long-lasting effects that it brings about in the psychical organization. In economic terms, the trauma is characterized by an influx of excitations that is excessive by the standard of the subject's tolerance and capacity to master such excitations and work them out psychically.

—Jean LaPlanche & Jean-Bertrand Pontalis, 1973

Bookends

*They are no lonelier than
a solitary slat on the bottom bunk of a bed
lamenting coil and fabric
who, in equal parts,
is resistant and obedient to the weight
of a single man,*
    clinging to the plunder of a proxy war.

*Nor are they as lonesome as
a stag patent leather pump
partner and resident starved
who, nursing the wound of injury and insult,
is a crumb of detritus
in a bouquet in a box,*
    overlooking the skeleton protruding from a carrion city.

Entertainment is the prolongation of work under late capitalism. [...] Even during their leisure time, consumers must orient themselves according to the unity of production.

—Theodor Adorno & Max Horkheimer, 1947

Kuya died from cardiac arrest while sitting in his armchair, watching breaking-news coverage of the eruption of Mt. Pinatubo on a local station in California. He made a widow out of Ate and she never remarried.

Chronic sighs, terminal sighs, swishing newspaper pages, barely audible condolences, shaking heads, harried remittances on a fax machine, humming fish-filled freezers, crumpling plastic grocery bags turned trash can liners, and jostled rosary beads—all wending through the three aisles of my grandparent's Asian grocery store.

This is the raucous melody emanating through the crack under the door that opens to my youth. Some philosopher said that the womb is louder, though.

This one made my hands filthy, as well.

Empty handed I entered the world/
Barefoot I leave it/
My coming, my going—
Two simple happenings, that got entangled

—Kozan Ichikyo, 1360

> As the dew appears/
> As the dew disappears/
> Such is my life, that Naniwa/
> Is a dream within a dream

—Toyotomi Hideyoshi, ca. 1575

> On a journey, ill/
> My dream goes wandering/
> Over withered fields

—Matsuo Basho, 1694

Northern Harrier

Heavy limb.
Heavy limbs.

Thick exhalation and unhurried effervescence.
Extant vitality bubbles out of a valve that wasn't there before.

The noonday devil is in league with the carbonated honey.

Bodhi Day is a Buddhist holiday that celebrates the day that Siddhartha Gautama became Buddha Shakyamuni after he achieved enlightenment while meditating beneath a fig tree.

There are two Bodhi Days. The first, sometimes referred to as "secular" Bodhi Day, which is observed the same day every year: December 8. The second Bodhi Day follows the lunar calendar and is celebrated on the eighth day after the twelfth new moon of the year.

At lolo's funeral, his brothers from the Masonic lodge came and administered to him what I assume is the Masonic equivalent of one's last rites.

I don't remember any of the prayer or incantation or whatever it is that they said. And I can barely remember if they all had on their little white aprons.

I do remember the single little sprig of evergreen they placed in his casket. It was pristine and balanced—five needle-adorned, finger-length, diminutive branches symmetrically emerging from a small, but substantial stem. It was almost uncanny, yet I was sure it had been alive on its coniferous mother earlier that morning.

I do remember how new it looked, there next to my old, dead lolo, dressed in his Barong Tagalog.

There was a celebration in town to-day because the Queen's message was received in the Atlantic cable. Guns were fired and church bells rung and flags were waving everywhere. In the evening there was torchlight procession . . . Grandfather says he thinks the 19th Psalm is a prophecy of the electric telegraph. "Their line is gone through all of the earth and their words to the end of the world." It certainly sounds like it.

—[unnamed sixteen-year-old girl's diary entry, August 16, 1858]

I don't remember exactly why I decided to try a sensory-deprivation float tank—I think I was trying to find a way to relax my muscles.

Before I closed the door to the tank, I wondered if I would be consumed by anxiety and let my thoughts abscond with me.

Once I found myself floating in the embrace of leaden darkness and syrupy silence, I felt my lower-back muscles release. Then I felt my jaw muscles relax. Then the muscles beneath my scalp.

I was full and hollow all at once, suspended in the exquisite absence of light. No frightening thoughts or silhouettes of nightmares. No ruminations, only questions to which I'll never seek answers:

Is this what astronauts feel like in zero gravity?

Was I in utero the last time I floated in the dark?

Could my ghost survive in outer space?

Could his?

The legend of the aswang existed prior to Spanish colonization. She is a specific kind of ghoul—and it is always a *she*.

By night, the creature separates her torso from her legs and sprouts wings. She is said to have a long, prehensile, barbed tongue, used specifically for piercing a body to suck out its viscera. She is particularly fond of amnion and is known to target pregnant women.

Gmail inbox ads tried to sell me the same leather handbag for twenty-nine out of thirty of the days in November.

(I don't know what happened on just that one day.)

• Can meaningful political debates be based on 280-character short messages? ... Short text invites simplistic arguments, and is an expression of the commodification, superficiality, tabloidization, and acceleration of culture.

—Christian Fuchs, 2021

Portrait of a Cultural Accelerant.

Lolo's casket was placed on the east end of the funeral home, while lola's was on the west. At her funeral service, some people complained that lola's makeup looked odd—too much rouge, perhaps. When I peered into her casket, I had to agree.

As odd as she looked, it somehow wasn't wrong.

After all, this was the woman who, through suffocating laughter, told me the story of when she was a teenager, and she and her sister went out to buy false eyelashes for attracting husbands. They acquired the eyelashes but didn't realize they needed eyelash glue to adhere them to their lash lines. Necessity is the mother of invention, and this was no different in Bulacan in the mid-twentieth century: the sisters went out back behind their house, not to a secret stash of cosmetics, but to a tree. A tree oozing sap. Sticky sap. Free sap. Lola and her sister used found tree sap to affix false lashes to their faces. I can only assume it worked.

Lola died a few weeks after dad.

I rode the train by myself to her funeral. On the way, I put on my makeup then handwrote her eulogy in a blue notebook.

The lotus flower is an icon and metaphor of enlightenment for two reasons:

> 1) Its seed can only germinate in the darkness of the mud at the bottom of relatively shallow bodies of water.
> 2) Its petals open one by one.

Today is Bodhi Day and the closest I am to enlightenment under a fig tree is my proximity to a two pack of Fig Newtons wallowing in the bottom of my purse.

Astronauts in microgravity experience a slew of physiological changes, including things like fluid rushing to the head and face, bone density deterioration, and muscle and connective tissue loss. Accordingly, astronauts have a rigid and rigorous fitness protocol to mitigate these effects. On the International Space Station, every astronaut spends, on average, about two hours per day exercising on the station's stationary bike, treadmill, and a specially designed weight lifting apparatus called the ARED (Advanced Resistive Exercise Device).

Outside the local library.

Pantoum 1A

There's a two-way tie for worst place:
A low-fuel light and a check-engine light.
There's a 7.9-billion-way tie for worst place—
Or at least that's the total, last time I checked.

A low-fuel light and a check-engine light—
They can exist at the same time and often do.
At least the last time I checked,
A wick can dangle out of both ends of a candle.

They can exist at the same time and often do,
not unlike squares and rectangles.
A wick does dangle out of both ends of a candle,
But that doesn't mean you should light them both.

Not unlike squares and rectangles,
There's a two-way tie for worst place.
You still shouldn't light them both, since
there's a 7.9-billion-way tie for worst place.

The subject of a controlled burn.

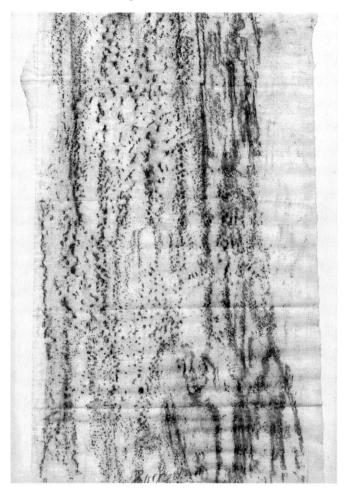

Telogen effluvium is the condition where hair follicles are rendered dormant after a period of high stress. The follicles' dormancy eventually causes the entire hair to fall out—usually a few weeks or months after the stressful occurrence.

I watched a TV show where a group of tourists were asked by their tour guide what they thought the lowest-status job in medieval continental Europe was. Almost all the people in the group, including some children, responded: a gravedigger. The tour guide jokingly replied that, no, it was actually the executioner who had the lowest-status job, but the gravedigger was a close second—and that they shared the same clientele. To which everyone in the tour group laughed.

What the guide neglected to tell them is this: to this day, the executioner still has the lowest-status job. The status has nothing to do with the compensation. In prisons where executions take place, it is not uncommon for a warden to hire an anonymous person to 'flip the switch' on fatal injections. This executioner is paid in cash and never asked their name.

The classified ad is the postmodern hangman's hood.

100.04

Zen Buddhist monks developed the haiku as a means of imparting wisdom. Many haiku writers over the ages have used a *saijiki* or an almanac of season-words to inform their poetry. A *saijiki* is best described as a haiku manual; it contains words belonging to broad categories of the subject matter of haiku, including seasons, humanity, observances, plants, animals, and the earth, sky, and elements.

Perhaps, above all else, the haiku is a microcosm of impermanence; its profoundly finite form that reflects back the vastness of our natural world is a reminder of both the brevity and beauty of life.

Perhaps the worst part of being half Western and half Eastern is that you have two pantheons of horrible creatures that haunt your childhood or await you in death.

I had two boogeymen, elbowing each other for space under my bed. There may have been up to four in the house at one time: two more in the next room over, silently fighting over the makeshift peephole crack of the closet door, waiting for my brother to fall asleep.

I wonder if his mumus *were watching when he slipped into death, there on his bed.*

Originally launched in 1977 to capture images of Jupiter and Saturn, the twin Voyager 1 and 2 spacecrafts also included a gold-plated copper record with playback instructions engraved in images and binary code upon its surface. The record includes over one hundred images and the sounds of human greetings in fifty-five languages and was intended to communicate the diversity of life on our planet to an extraterrestrial audience.

Carl Sagan, who chaired the committee that decided the content of the golden record, noted: "The spacecraft will be encountered, and the record played only if there are advanced spacefaring civilizations in interstellar space."

100.05

My mother was twenty-three when she birthed me and about thirty-five when she started to notice grey hairs. Sometimes she would ask me to tweeze her grey hairs, which I happily obliged for two reasons that I didn't understand at the time: I had trichotillomania and it was the only time I felt close to her. We would get on her and dad's bed, and after selecting precisely the right TV show that required only a portion of our attention, she would rest her head on my lap, and I'd get to work. I feel her hair in mine now.

The Gothics set stone upon stone, ever higher, not, as the giants did, to attack God, but to reach up to Him. And God, as in the German legend, rewarded the merchants and the warriors, but to the poet, what was granted?

> "Where were you at the time of the distribution? I did not see you, poet."
> "Lord, I was at your feet."
> "Then sometime you shall come up beside me."

Thus it was the poet who guided the masterbuilder, and in reality the poet built the Cathedral.

—Auguste Rodin, 1914

When I don't think about technology, I think about animals.

My husband is a semiotician, and he studies the people who study animal cognition. He has lots to say about the difference between humans and animals.

> *My only thought on the matter:*
> *Humans are the only animal who know they are going to die.*

Flyers removed with fire.

"Ennui the Chief Incentive to Drink"

—*New York Tribune* headline, May 28, 1899

My brother and I were made responsible for disseminating flyers around our neighborhood for our father's lawn-care business. They were small quarter sheets that we rolled up and stuck in the metalwork of storm doors, jambs, and even the miniscule curves of the handles of mailboxes, careful not to put them inside the mailbox, because they were not technically mail.

The wind picked up that day and some of the flyers ended up blowing away. A neighborhood grouch called the number on the flyer and said we were littering. My mother received the call before we even returned home.

We were sent out again to pick up the scattered flyers.

—

Tape this note to your computer monitor:
Tu se' Pagliaccio/
Vesti la giubba/
E la faccia infarina/
La gente paga.

The International Space Station orbits the Earth at around 28,000 km/h.

The Earth moves around the sun at over 100,000 km/h.

The sun moves around the center of the Milky Way galaxy at around 230 km/s.

The Milky Way galaxy moves at around 550 km/s.

Sometime after the fall of the Berlin Wall and shortly before the total dissolution of the Soviet Union, I saw a ghost, or at least I think I saw a ghost. Kid brains are funny like that.

I was playing and running around my lolo and lola's house, trying to keep up with my brother and older cousins. Their legs were longer therefore, they had more fun. We wove in and out of grown-ups and furniture until it was time to take the fun downstairs to the basement. Like I said, I had the shortest legs, since little Cindy hadn't come along quite yet, and my legs felt even shorter when going down lolo and lola's seemingly gargantuan basement stairs. I remember that the stairs had grey paint on them, which was thoroughly chipped, revealing an older rusty red coat of paint and in places, the bare board itself. I'd study these stairs in the years after the sighting since I became too afraid to look up while I made the descent into the basement.

I don't remember much before or after I started screaming, but I saw something while I clung tight to the banister and carefully placed one foot after another on each stair. The sloping ceiling above the stairs was incomplete. You could see drywall, unfinished wood, and some of the cotton candy insulation, all thanks to a precarious little light bulb screwed into one of the exposed boards. There, betwixt some insulation and two-by-fours, I saw something. I thought I saw something. A face then a head emerged from the darkness and caught a touch of the feeble light. It was a man's face. He had a widow's peak with dark hair and pale skin, yet it was a manufactured paleness: he wore caked-on white makeup with smears of light blue and some pink around his mouth. Perhaps the makeup had been violently smeared by someone or something because I do remember some of his cheek skin was sloughing or hanging off, as though he had been the victim of a botched flaying or a gruesome animal attack.

He smiled and I screamed.

And I screamed and screamed until lolo came and scooped me up off the stairs.

I figured it was a young, impressionable mind that had cooked up this specter, complete with the hairline of Bela Lugosi, the clown makeup of Pennywise, and the mangled, disfigured visage of a man mauled by a werewolf. I told myself that I made it all up, especially when I would rush downstairs to grab lola's laundry from the dryer in the basement. I even assured myself that I had made it up when lolo and lola finally had the ceiling above the stairs finished and sealed off.

One time I jokingly told my brother that I thought I saw something in lolo and lola's basement. He jokingly told me that one time he heard a voice from the open basement door. I didn't really want to know what the voice said, but he told me anyway.

"Psst. Come over here."

I suppose I've known the face of his mumu *all along, and he'd only known the sound. To be sure, it was never my* mumu—*it had always been his.*

The demon of . . . [acedia], also called "the noonday demon," . . . is the most oppressive of all demons. He attacks the monk about the fourth hour and besieges his soul until the eighth hour. First he makes the sun appear sluggish and immobile, as if the day had fifty hours . . . He stirs the monk also to long for . . . a much less toilsome and more expedient profession . . . To these thoughts the demon adds the memory of the monk's family and of his former way of life.

—Evagrius Ponticus, ca. 375 CE

I may need electroconvulsive therapy (ECT) later this year because I have exhausted the other treatment options for major depressive disorder (MDD).

A primary risk of ECT is memory loss. Risk or benefit—I am not entirely sure.

I read about ECT sometimes—google it, even. So now the archive that exists solely for advertisements directed at me tries to sell me treatments for MDD. At times, ads for pharmaceuticals almost seem compassionate. The way they appear in the margins of web pages and between paragraphs about neurotransmitters and how ECT is not a gruesome procedure reserved for the asylums of old.

They never feel so compassionate that I want to ask my doctor about it, though.

The three main threats to human health in the vacuum of space are variable gravity, lack of oxygen, and radiation. If sucked out of an airlock in low Earth orbit without a space suit, a human body would expand (but not explode since skin elasticity accommodates this growth), be knocked unconscious due to lack of oxygen within mere seconds, then experience complete brain death a few minutes afterward. Variable gravity has health effects ranging from space adaptation syndrome (much like motion sickness on Earth), to rapid muscle atrophy, to supporting the growth of antibiotic-resistant bacteria in an individual's gut. Finally, though the sample size is limited to the twenty-four Apollo lunar astronauts who are the only humans to have left the protection of Earth's magnetosphere, exposure to deep-space cosmic radiation has been linked to a dramatically increased risk for mortality related to cardiovascular disease.

—

Hum:
The *"mmm, mmm, mmm, mm-mm-m-mm-mm"* at the beginning of Simon & Garfunkel's "America."

Posting for a lost dog.

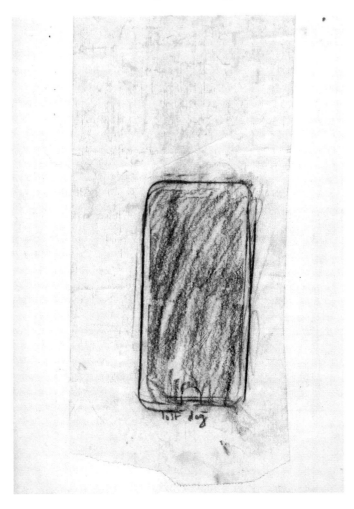

My brother was a nineteen-year-old drug addict. He popped and snorted prescription pills, any pills, really, and experimented with intravenous heroin. When he got in trouble with the law and had to submit weekly drug tests, he drank over-the-counter cough syrup because it doesn't show up in urinalysis.

I couldn't really understand the tox report from his autopsy because there were so many different drugs in his system when he died, though I suppose that's all there is to understand: he took all of them. On purpose.

Since his death, I've far exceeded the amount of prescription drugs that he could have taken in his brief life, though mine were given to me by a doctor and I can't stop taking them. On purpose.

Anhedonia is a psychological condition characterized by an inability to experience pleasure in normally pleasurable acts.

A couple of weeks before the wedding, the bride started packing up her room. The swishing of cardboard pushed across cardboard muffled the sound of her arrival—the bride barely heard when she came by and roosted on the windowsill. They only greeted each other and had some small talk. She didn't help pack or sort. She had plenty of time to ask the bride for her new address or where she was going, but she didn't. She knew the bride wouldn't divulge that to her, especially after she was caught examining the birth control pills in her purse, trying to figure out her menstrual cycle.

When she leaned back and popped open her leathery wings to depart, she was upset and wearing a rare expression: an inflamed amalgamation of resentment and longing. The bride had seen it only once before, during senior year of high school when she told her that she had had an abortion.

That night was the last time they spoke, though the bride did see her perched in the tree outside her window the night before the wedding. They made eye contact, but she never paused twisting her stringy, etiolated tongue around one of her claws, as if it were a strand of hair.

"Longtermism" is a scientistic pseudophilosophy that entails that nothing matters unless it is an existential threat to the human species, and that we are indebted to a future about which we know nothing. Longtermists purposely overlook the social, political, and economic problems of today, deeming them unworthy of fixing because their presence will not obstruct our species continuation.

I still listen to the radio.

I still listen to the radio because I become overwhelmed trying to choose something to listen to on music streaming services. I've heard this called "decision fatigue."

I still listen to the radio and sometimes I hear ads for local addiction services.

    I still listen to the radio because dad pressed the presets on my car radio, too.

His Holiness the Fourteenth Dalai Lama suggests that happiness is our default setting and that the entire point of life is to return to this happiness. He also suggests that our underlying human nature is one of gentleness and compassion.

At thirty-five years old, I never see the mumu *or boogeyman under the bed I share with my spouse. I never see them, but I know they are there.*

They leave their molted hair behind. Their hair that is the same texture as each other's, and the same texture as mine. It is everywhere, mixed with dust and clothing lint, and it swirls and writhes when I exhale with my cheek pressed on the floor, looking for something that I have already forgotten.

The sensation of weightlessness was somewhat unusual compared to ground conditions. Here a sensation arose like hanging horizontally on belts, as if in a suspended state. Evidently, the tightly fitted harness system exerts pressure on the rib cage, and therefore creates the impression that you're hanging. Then you become accustomed and adapt to this. There were no bad sensations.

—Major Yuri Gagarin, 1961

An ad for an SSRI before it scampered away.

Lola's Superstitions: Greatest Hits Vol. I

–Don't go to sleep with wet hair, you'll get sick
–Don't go outside with wet hair, you'll get sick
–Don't braid your hair when it's wet, you'll turn all your hair white and then it will fall out
–Only wear real 24K gold, or else you'll get struck by lightning
–Ay nako! Don't talk about death, it's bad luck
–Don't pull out a white hair because two will grow back in its place
–Don't step on anthills because duwendes live in there and they'll curse you if you disturb their home
–Pray to Saint Anthony (. . . or is it Saint Joseph?) if you can't find your jewelry
–Her purse is definitely a knockoff—not mine, though
–Never gift a watch or clock to your lover because it will count down the time you have together
–Never take the last piece of food—offer it to someone else

100.06

A "sky burial" is a funerary practice by Tibetan Buddhists in which the body of the deceased is left out for carrion-eating animals to consume, as opposed to a burial in earth or cremation. The *tokden*, or sky-burial master, is responsible for cutting up remains to facilitate efficient disposal by attracting vultures. The *tokden* is not a priest or a shaman; a tokden's role is not to help a soul through the bardo and into its next life and body. A *tokden* is concerned with remains and is most closely aligned with a butcher while sharing the same social status.

I have been dismissed by Gen Z colleagues on several occasions when asking them questions about this or that. They've said, "I dunno. Just google it," not understanding that I was trying to have a friendly conversation. They don't know how to respond when I tell them I use google sparingly.

Informed by my willingness to wait, and my fondness for my very own ad-free data and memory apparatus, my praxis is this:
    1) If I knew something at one point in time, it probably lives in my brain somewhere, and I might come upon it later when I think an adjacent thought.
    2) If I never knew something at any point in time, and only want to know for the sake of chitchat, I wait and watch the desire to know recede like the wave upon which it crashed.

Among my younger peers, it remains unclear if I am a conversation-starter or -ender.

In the Tibetan Book of the Dead, one of the six classes of beings inhabiting the desire realm (*our* realm) are *anguished spirits,* or spirit beings who are under the sway of attachment and unsatisfied craving.

Adjacent to a recently demolished historic home.

100.07

I had a miscarriage when my father was having his tongue cut out in the hospital. I did not tell him what happened, and he went to his grave not knowing. I wish every day that the baby would've survived so my father could have met his grandchild. I was too scared to even think about children immediately after his death, and I still don't know how to bring a life into a sparse and imploded family. When I think about children now, all I imagine is a single cell beginning to replicate in the sea billions of years ago.

After the 1859 Carrington Event, there was one case of an unplugged telegraph machine that continued operating because it was powered by a rogue current in the atmosphere.

100.08

I am in constant search of rib-sticking wisdom that might help me better make sense of my chronic ennui. I read in one of my Buddhist magazines that one might imagine a computer or a smartphone as a prosthetic mind or brain. My ribs felt plumper, filled out, as though they had gone through puberty after I had read this short article. Alas, in the weeks after I read this, I chewed the sinews off my sternum when I found that, even with the help of a prosthesis, I had no strength for the agony of absence in two places.

The sixth [devil] was called *silagan*, whose office it was, if they saw anyone clothed in white, to tear out his liver and eat it, thus causing his death. This, like the preceding, was in the island of Catanduanes. Let no one, moreover, consider this a fable; because, in Calavan, they tore out in this way through the anus all the intestines of a Spanish notary, who was buried in Calilaya by Father Fray Juan de Mérida.

The seventh [devil] was called *magtatangal*, and his purpose was to show himself at night to many persons, without his head or entrails. In such wise the devil walked about and carried, or pretended to carry, his head to different places; and, in the morning, returned it to his body—remaining, as before, alive. This seems to me to be a fable, although the natives affirm that they have seen it, because the devil probably caused them so to believe. This occurred in Catanduanes.

The eighth [devil] they called *osuang*, which is equivalent to "sorcerer;" they say that they have seen him fly, and that he murdered men and ate their flesh. This was among the Visayas Islands; among the Tagalos these did not exist.

—Friar Juan de Plasencia, Order of Saint Francis, ca. 1577

I had an art teacher in high school who, every Thursday, made my class do contour line drawing. She would create a display of varied objects with distinct shapes and textures; I remember fruits, helmets, and opened boxes heaped on a table in the middle of the classroom. She instructed us to pick an object or area on the table, put our pencil to paper, and draw it with a single line.

She insisted we not look down at our papers or pencils. Absolutely no picking up the pencil—pencil always to paper, no sketching. She insisted for an entire semester.

After a few Thursdays, we were allowed to glance down, only briefly, at our paper. But if we held our gaze too long, she would interrupt:

> The information you need is not on the paper.
> Look at *what* you're drawing, not the drawing itself.

Tips for monetizing one's social media.

It's estimated that that kind of event right now would be catastrophic across the globe. That means no Internet, no phone, no TV, and no power. And not just that—even, like, the water-cleaning systems and health systems—all those things could be potentially wiped out. Anything with an electrical circuit could be potentially destroyed. You know, some people have estimated it would take us years to recover—ten years to recover from one storm like that.

—Dr. Samaiyah Farid, 2022

When I first learned of my brother's death, I sprinted into myself.

She sprints and I walk. She's so much faster than me.

I am searching for her, but the trail has gone cold—the archive, dried up.
Google is no help.
Facebook is no help.
Do they still put missing children on the sides of milk cartons? Or will this take a conjuring?

Somewhere, there she is—leaning on a lightning-struck lamppost, the sign of the cross smeared on her forehead with volcanic ash.

Somewhere, there I am—my right hand thumbing beads on a japamala, my left hand pressing Ctrl+F.

Somewhere, here she is—searching for a charging outlet beneath the headless body of Ferdinand Magellan.

Somewhere, here I am—still winded and second windless, doubled over inside of a rumination.

Morning sun in springtime

Acknowledgments

For their guidance and support on this project, I gratefully acknowledge Elisabeth Sheffield, Julie Carr, and Kelly Hurley. I also thank Caleb Tardío and Katy Rossing, whose patience, affirmation, and love gave me the fortitude to see this through.